Kosher Lutherans

by William Missouri Downs

A SAMUEL FRENCH ACTING EDITION

SAMUEL FRENCH

FOUNDED 1830

NEW YORK HOLLYWOOD LONDON TORONTO

SAMUELFRENCH.COM

ISBN 978-0-573-69715-9   Printed in U.S.A.   #29131

IMPORTANT BILLING AND CREDIT
REQUIREMENTS

All producers of *KOSHER LUTHERANS must* give credit to the Author of the Play in all programs distributed in connection with performances of the Play, and in all instances in which the title of the Play appears for the purposes of advertising, publicizing or otherwise exploiting the Play and/or a production. The name of the Author *must* appear on a separate line on which no other name appears, immediately following the title and *must* appear in size of type not less than fifty percent of the size of the title type.

KOSHER LUTHERANS was originally produced by the University of Wyoming's Summer Theatre in 2007. The cast and crew was as follows:

FRANKLYN . . . . Wolf J. Sherrill
HANNAH. . . . . Anna Brownsted
BEN . . . . Michael James Smith
MARTHA. . . . . Dodie Montgomery
ALISON . . . . Rachel Rosenfeld

Director – William Missouri Downs
Scene Design – Michael Earl
Lighting Design – Adam Mendelson
Costume Design – Ellen Bredehoft
Sound Design – Adam Mendelson
Production Stage Manager – Catherine Wallis

Special Thanks to: Lou Anne Wright, Chameleon Playwrights of Denver, Michael Earl, Adam Mendelson, Catherine Wallis, and Gwen Feldman.

CAST OF CHARACTERS
(2 MEN – 3 WOMEN)

FRANKLYN - (A Perfect Husband – late thirties)
HANNAH - (A Perfect Wife – late thirties)
BEN - (An Imperfect Husband – late thirties)
MARTHA - (An Imperfect Wife – late thirties)
ALISON - (An eighteen-year-old girl from Iowa)

SETTING

Franklyn & Hannah's living room & dining room table

PLACE

Van Nuys, California

TIME

Act One – Purim
Act Two, Scene One – The first night of Hanukkah
Act Two, Scene Two – A month later

ACT ONE

Purim

(**FRANKLYN** *sits alone in the living room reading from his manuscript.*)

FRANKLYN. "She strolls in for dinner like a centipede with 92 legs missing. Her eyes were as dark as new tires yet they flashed like luminous hubcaps, while her hair gently rolled down her shoulders exactly the way a bowling ball wouldn't. 'What's for dinner' she said, her lips forming a perfect oval, like a circle compressed by a Thigh Master." ...Wow. That's good.

(**HANNAH** *enters dressed for a dinner party and sets the table. She is running late.*)

I mean that's really quite good.

HANNAH. *(busy – not listening)* Yes dear.

FRANKLYN. I guess it's time I admit it to myself. I'm a writer!

HANNAH. Would you open the wine?

FRANKLYN. This night school professor says to me, in front of the entire class, she says my opening scene can't take place at a dinner party – No dinner scenes allowed. Says all they do is make people hungry

HANNAH. *(not paying attention)* That's nice dear.

FRANKLYN. Instead she thinks it should take place someplace exciting, like a doctor's waiting room with a dentist drill screaming in the background. Or the burning deck of an aircraft carrier under Kamikaze attack. But if you think about it Kamikaze attack or dinner party – Kamikaze attack – dinner party. Obviously a dinner party would be far more interesting. Let me read it again. "She walks in for dinner like a centipede with 94 legs missing –."

HANNAH. I know your creative juices are flowing right now, but they'll be here any minute.

FRANKLYN. No they won't. They're always late.

HANNAH. You don't know that.

FRANKLYN. And all they do is talk about things.

HANNAH. That's what couples do when they get together, they talk about things.

FRANKLYN. No, I mean *things*. Last time he spent thirty minutes discussing his new, "top of the top" of the line, 60,000 BTU Weber grill with automatic moistness control. And always a new car – Every eighteen months – spanking brand new car.

HANNAH. It makes them happy – So what.

FRANKLYN. Know why we're friends? Cause his name is Ben and I'm Franklyn. That's it, that's what our entire friendship is based on. Ben. Franklyn. Back in college, we thought it was cool – Used to go to bars and pick up history majors.

(HANNAH grabs BEN's manuscript and exits.)

FRANKLYN. Hey, I'm not done –

HANNAH *(offstage)* Is that what you two were up to the other night? You came in awfully late.

FRANKLYN. What's this?

HANNAH *(offstage)* After your writing class you said you bumped into Ben.

FRANKLYN. Oh, right, after class, right –. *(notices the mezuzah on the door frame)* What's that?

(HANNAH enters with dinner party snacks.)

HANNAH. Huh?

FRANKLYN. That?

HANNAH. It's a mezuzah.

FRANKLYN. Doesn't it go on the outside?

HANNAH. I know but Bubbe gave it to me and it's so pretty I thought I'd glue it to the inside.

FRANKLYN. Glue? You used glue?

HANNAH. Removable permanent glue. Open the wine.

FRANKLYN. Removable permanent – Who ever heard of such a thing?

HANNAH. Would you open the wine. They'll be here any moment.

(**FRANKLYN** *opens a bottle of wine.* **HANNAH** *puts the finishing touches on the table.*)

FRANKLYN. You know, maybe it's not such a good idea to have them over for Purim? They are raging alcoholics.

HANNAH. They're not alcoholics. They hardly drink at all.

FRANKLYN. Then how come they constantly fight? It's like having an opera in our living room without the music.

HANNAH. Little love spats, it's nothing.

FRANKLYN. And if you want my opinion, she's a little wacky.

HANNAH. Watch it, she's my cousin.

FRANKLYN. Distant cousin – From the wacky-raging-alco-holic-fighting side of the family.

HANNAH. She's been a little depressed since Isaac's death –.

FRANKLYN. It's been three years.

HANNAH. Why're you bringing this up? Have you changed your mind? You don't want to ask them?

FRANKLYN. What? No. I'm fine with asking.

HANNAH. You sure?

FRANKLYN. Totally fine.

HANNAH. Cause if you really think they're wacky alcohol-ics –.

FRANKLYN. I'm fine…Cause I have no doubt they're going to totally freak out.

HANNAH. You don't know that.

FRANKLYN. Yes I do. He'll have to consult with the highest rabbinical authorities before he says "no" and she'll say "no" cause she's afraid of needles – mark my words.

HANNAH. How do you know she's afraid of needles?

FRANKLYN. Trust me, now that I'm a writer I'm a great judge of character.

HANNAH. Let's not second guess life.

(She kisses him on the cheek.)

(doorbell)

HANNAH. That's them.

FRANKLYN. And only twenty minutes late. Everything's Kosher, right?

HANNAH. Mostly – why?

FRANKLYN. I just don't want another Cheez-it incident.

(an offstage bing)

HANNAH. Oh, that's the oven. Get the door.

(HANNAH runs into the kitchen. FRANKLYN heads for the door.)

FRANKLYN. Idea! *(calling off to HANNAH)* What if I switch and have the opening scene take place in a stuck subway car?

HANNA *(Offstage)* Get the door!

FRANKLYN. You got your darkness, your menacing third rail, and no food, she's gotta love that...

(FRANKLYN opens the door to find BEN with two bottles of wine.)

BEN. Happy Purim fella!

FRANKLYN. Ben.

BEN. Franklyn!

(BEN hugs FRANKLYN.)

FRANKLYN. Where's Martha?

BEN. Parking. Took separate cars. She bought a new S.U.V. – insisted on driving. Told her parking in Van Nuys is a pain in the butt – that we'd have a better chance finding a spot with my BMW – had a fight, took separate cars, what's for din?

FRANKLYN. Sorry to hear that.

BEN. Told her not to buy a Caddy – Did she listen? The gas mileage of an M-1 tank. But it does have dual temperature controls. You gotta have dual temperature controls, life is too short to live without dual temperature controls.

(**HANNAH** *enters with fresh out of the oven Haman's pockets.*)

HANNAH. Ben.

BEN. The other half of the perfect couple!

(**BEN** *hugs* **HANNAH.**)

HANNAH. Where's Martha?

BEN. Parking her new Cadillac S.U.V. – the best of the best.

FRANKLYN. Dual temperature controls, sweetheart.

HANNAH. Dual temperature, imagine that.

BEN. Told her not to bring it. Had a fight. What's it been two years?

HANNAH. I think you're right two years.

BEN. And still no children?

HANNAH. Thanks for bringing it up, but you're right, still no children.

BEN. Still trying?

HANNAH. We never stop trying.

FRANKLYN. *(changing the subject)* So Ben, how's business?

BEN. Making a killing. *(to* **HANNAH***)* Have you tried in vitro fertilization?

FRANKLYN. Wine?

BEN. Cause if you haven't I know this doctor – Doctor Arnold Rosen –.

HANNAH. Yes, you suggested him two years ago.

BEN. Has a seventy-five-point-four percent success rate. You'll be pregnant so fast your head'll spin. He's Martha's gynecologist.

FRANKLYN. *(again, trying to change the subject)* I decided on Chardonnay. The L.A. Times said that this one has a sweet citrus taste complemented by a touch of spicy oak.

(**FRANKLYN** *pours wine.*)

BEN. You know a few months ago Martha and I thought about having a kid.

HANNAH. Really?

BEN. We were watching TV on our 52-inch plasma – you gotta get one of these Frankie – great color and depth, I swear the screen has depth – when we suddenly realized that we got enough money, a great house and the schools are kinda close. It's a perfect situation for children. So we resolved to go upstairs and get started, knowwhatImean?

HANNAH. Ben, Martha never told me this.

BEN. Then we got really interested in this episode of Seinfeld and forgot. I swear we forgot. Totally and completely forgot.

HANNAH. Then perhaps it's best that you don't have children.

BEN. You know, I've found that couples who want kids but can't have 'em often have serious long lasting issues with depression. Then hostility sets in, pressure from family and before you know it the marriage is in the toilet. If you're interested, I know this head doctor who specializes in childless couples. Got his card here some place.

(**BEN** *digs into his business card wallet.*)

FRANKLYN. *(changing the subject)* So how's that Weber working out?

BEN. Oh! Cooked on it yesterday. You know the word "cooked" is just too crude to describe the experience. I *created* on it. *(to* **HANNAH**, *handing her the card)* Dr. Frank Green. He counsels bunches of those anorexic Hollywood starlets who can't have kids cause all they eat is organic soy-crap and lime-water. *(to* **FRANKLYN***)* It's called XR-73. Remember that XR-73. Let me write it down for you. *(He writes it on the back of the business card.)* – You gotta get one of these – It's got 60,000 BTUs and automatic moistness control.

FRANKLYN. I'm not so much into moistness.

BEN. Top of the top of the line. Got 'em only at special stores in affluent neighborhoods – near movie stars and whatever.

HANNAH. And there is one near you?

BEN. No. I heard about it from Doctor Rosen – Did you know that he once got a fifty-six year-old woman pregnant – course that had nothing to do with in vitro hence the lawsuit.

(doorbell)

HANNAH. She found a spot.

(HANNAH *heads for the door.)*

BEN. Hannah, before you let her in do me a favor will ya?

HANNAH. Sure.

BEN. I know this is going to upset you but…Martha and I… we…maybe you should sit down for this.

(doorbell)

HANNAH. Can I get the door first?

BEN. I guess I'll just say it. Martha and I…we…decided to call it splits.

HANNAH. What?

BEN. I know I know – long story – just don't bring it up in front of her.

FRANKLYN. Ben, what're you saying?

BEN. Contacted a lawyer friend this morning.

HANNAH. Ben, I'm –.

BEN. Totally shocked. I know, you thought we were the perfect couple. Isn't that strange, we thought *you* were the perfect couple.

HANNAH. But you've been married for so long –.

BEN. Not that long – six years. She didn't want you to know, being that you introduced us. I insisted we be up front. She didn't think it was a good idea. Had a fight.

(two doorbells)

FRANKLYN. What're we supposed to do?

BEN. Just act like I didn't tell you.

FRANKLYN. Then why did you tell us?

(three doorbells)

BEN. Everything'll be fine. We'll drink some wine and have a great time. Just don't make us sit next to each other. Or near each other for that matter.

HANNAH. Maybe we should call this off.

FRANKLYN. Yes, that does seem best –.

BEN. Look, if you're going to make a big deal out of it –.

HANNAH. It is a big deal.

BEN. We're getting divorced; it's not the end of the world. The sun turning into a red giant and crashing into Krakatoa – that's the end of the world, this is nothing more than a blip.

*(The door pops open. It's **MARTHA**.)*

MARTHA. What, are we not answering doorbells today?

HANNAH. Martha!

MARTHA. I rang and rang.

HANNAH. I'm so sorry.

*(**FRANKLYN** helps **MARTHA** with her coat.)*

MARTHA. Frankie. Thank you. Such a gentleman.

HANNAH. Lovely dress.

MARTHA. Neiman Marcus. *(then she glares at **BEN**)* You took my parking spot.

BEN. It was way too small.

MARTHA. Even if it was, I saw it first.

BEN. So what. You couldn't fit.

MARTHA. You *assumed* I couldn't fit.

BEN. I had only inches to spare.

MARTHA. All I'm saying is that a gentleman would offer and not assume.

BEN. What type of offer is that? Here's a parking space that's much too small for your M1 S.U.V. – It's an empty gesture.

MARTHA. Empty or not, you should offer and not assume!

BEN. I wasn't assuming anything, I know what fits. I have spatial intelligence.

MARTHA. Spatial intelligence? What the hell is this spatial intelligence?

BEN. It's the talent to know what fits! And you don't got it.

MARTHA. All I'm saying is that a gentleman would offer!

BEN. Next time I'll make an empty gesture! Happy?

FRANKLYN. Wine?

MARTHA. Maybe there won't be a next time!

BEN. Fine! I'll gladly go out and move my Beemer! The offer's been made. Are we happy?! The keys are in my hand I will walk out there right now if you want! Are we happy? Answer the question, are we happy?!

MARTHA. Yes! We are happy!

BEN. Good!

(*Beat* – BEN *and* MARTHA *glare at each other.*)

FRANKLYN. …It has a citrus taste complemented by a touch of spicy –.

MARTHA. Sorry. Shalom.

HANNAH. Yes, Shalom.

(**FRANKLYN** *pours wine* – *They drink.* **BEN** *and* **MARTHA** *gulp.*)

BEN. More.

MARTHA. Same here.

(*They empty their glasses again. They start to sit next to each other on the couch.*)

HANNAH. Wait, we'll take the couch.

(**FRANKLYN** *and* **HANNAH** *scramble to sit center on the couch separating* **BEN** *and* **MARTHA**. *An uncomfortable pause.*)

BEN. (*to* **FRANKLYN**) …I barely fit. Had to go back and forth and back and forth and back and forth at least twenty times – I counted.

MARTHA. (*to* **HANNAH**) One shouldn't *assume* should one?

BEN. *(to* **FRANKLYN***)* Did you know that I have spatial intelligence?

HANNAH. How about a toast?

BEN. Sure.

MARTHA. Why not.

> *(They raise their glasses.)*

HANNAH. To…To…Friends.

> *(They toast.* **FRANKLYN** *and* **HANNAH** *sip.* **MARTHA** *and* **BEN** *down their glasses.)*

BEN. More.

MARTHA. Same here.

> *(***BEN** *and* **MARTHA** *down their glasses again. Another uncomfortable pause.)*

HANNAH. *(trying to be up beat)* Franklyn has good news.

MARTHA. *(jumping up)* No! No, no, no don't say it! It's true! I can see it in your eyes! You went to Dr. Rosen! Boy or Girl? Boy or Girl?

HANNAH. No –.

MARTHA. I knew this would happen! I knew it! I had a sick-headache today that always means good news is coming! Hannah I'm so happy for you – Oh, you shouldn't be drinking!

> *(***MARTHA** *downs* **HANNAH***'s wine.)*

HANNAH. But–

MARTHA. Trust me I know what I'm doing–

HANNAH. I'm not pregnant.

MARTHA. …You're not?

HANNAH. That's not the good news.

MARTHA. It's not?

HANNAH. No.

MARTHA. I'm so very sorry. I just assumed that–

BEN. You assumed! I thought people weren't supposed to assume?!

MARTHA. There are times when assuming is not an assumption!

BEN. An assumption is different from assuming?

MARTHA. Depending on the circumstances!

BEN. Circumstances! What circumstances? When is it okay to make our best friends feel like crap cause they can't have children?

MARTHA. It was a logical guess not an assumption! So shut your trap and settle!

BEN. Oh it's closed trust me it's closed!

MARTHA. Then close it and settle!

BEN. It's closed!

MARTHA. Settle!

(an uncomfortable pause)

HANNAH. ...What I was going to say is that Franklyn is taking six months off to write his novel.

BEN. Oh.

MARTHA. Nice.

(Beat. BEN puts his hand up.)

BEN. Question.

FRANKLYN. Sure.

BEN. What novel?

FRANKLYN. I've been working on this novel. Well, more like a novelette.

MARTHA. You mean like with words and pages?

FRANKLYN. And with some luck soon chapters.

BEN. Since when do you write?

FRANKLYN. I've been taking this night school class.

HANNAH. It's not going to be easy, but we can make it on one salary for a while...with some luck...And we, I mean Frankie, figured it's the perfect time to do it... Before we have children.

BEN. Wow. Ya think you know someone and suddenly they're writing a novelette.

MARTHA. Excuse me, I don't want to appear the least bit negative but I assume you've written before – ?

BEN. You assume?

MARTHA. Shut up and settle!

BEN. FINE!

MARTHA. SETTLE!

FRANKLYN. ...No. This'll be my first try.

HANNAH. That's not true. I fell in love with Frankie when he sent me a poem in college.

BEN. And the old man gave you six months off, you lucky dog.

HANNAH. No, he quit.

MARTHA. No way.

FRANKLYN. I came home the other night and began wondering what I was doing. Am I going to push papers for Hannah's father for the rest of my life? I've always wanted to be a writer but then reality set in. So the next day I stopped by this butcher shop, got myself a huge roll of paper, a la Jack Kerouac, found a pawnshop typewriter, called in sick and started typing.

BEN. What's it about?

FRANKLYN. *(to BEN)* Well, I'm kinda finding my way, but today it's about this trio of ambitious friends in Manhattan...

MARTHA. *(to HANNAH)* And you support this?

HANNAH. *(to MARTHA)* I don't think I have a choice.

FRANKLYN. *(to BEN)* ...The problem is they can't separate their professional and personal lives...

MARTHA. *(to HANNAH)* You don't sound too sure about this.

FRANKLYN. *(to BEN)* ...Then one day they, get this, they get stuck in this subway car...

HANNAH. *(to MARTHA)* Well, I don't know how we're going to make it.

FRANKLYN. *(to BEN)* ...Total darkness! The menacing third rail just inches away – !

HANNAH. *(to MARTHA)* Frankie sort of insisted.

BEN. ...Wait a minute, wait a minute! Frankie insisted? I see what happened here. You two had a fight. The perfect couple had a fight!

MARTHA. Ben, that's hardly nice.

BEN. Come on admit it. You had a fight. Just like Martha and me. Go on, admit it!

FRANKLYN. We had a discussion.

BEN. *(to MARTHA)* You're always telling me, "Why can't we be like Frankie and Hannah. They never fight."

MARTHA. I've never said such a thing. *(to HANNAH)* Rest assured, I know you two fight.

HANNAH. It wasn't really a fight.

BEN. No no no, don't disappoint me. Say it! Say it!

HANNAH. It was...It was...

BEN. Yes?

HANNAH. ...It was a fight.

(**BEN** *grabs the Purim Gragger [noisemaker] from the coffee table, gets up and does a little dance.*)

BEN. *(singsong)* They had a fight, they had a fight!

MARTHA. I am so sorry. Rest assured I do not condone my husband's behavior.

FRANKLYN. It wasn't really a fight. It was more like a discussion. Hannah?

HANNAH. No dear, it was more like a fight.

FRANKLYN. *(to BEN)* Would you please stop dancing.

BEN. I used to come to Frankie for advice about my marriage. Let me tell you he was always the expert. Always the A-number-one authority on marriage. *(beat – singsong)* But they had a fight!

MARTHA. You asked Franklyn advice about our marriage?

BEN. It was nothing, we'd get together and compare notes.

MARTHA. So what did he tell you?

FRANKLYN. *(trying to change the subject)* Ben, I was really thinking about getting an XR 37. Do they have a payment plan?

MARTHA. What do you know about our marriage?

FRANKLYN. I know nothing. Most of the time it was Dodgers talk.

BEN. And I always followed his advice. Web flowers Fridays. That was Frankie's idea.

MARTHA. You gave me web flowers every Friday on advice from a friend?

BEN. He used to send me reminder emails every Friday morning –.

HANNAH. Wait a minute. You advised Ben to send flowers to his wife every Friday?

FRANKLYN. Web flowers. Not real flowers –.

HANNAH. Don't I rate flowers?

FRANKLYN. Hannah, our marriage isn't in trouble.

BEN. It is now!

(**BEN** *does another little dance.*)

MARTHA. Well, I'm just humiliated, totally and completely humiliated. To think, I was coming over here, breaking bread with friends and you knew what was going on behind the closed doors of my marriage.

FRANKLYN. Look, everyone calm down. Sometimes men talk. We're not experts at being married. I've never been married before – Ben never. We…we…

BEN. Compared notes.

FRANKLYN. It's nothing personal. Ben asked my advice cause he mistakenly thought that I had a perfect marriage. Now please, if everyone will just…just…

MARTHA. Settle!

BEN. Yes! Settle…

(*They sit silent. They drink. Beat.*)

MARTHA. …I too have an announcement.

FRANKLYN. Oh god no.

MARTHA. This isn't easy. Since we moved to Westwood, we just don't keep up like we once did. Well, I want you to know there have been a few changes in my life. You know, there comes a point where you begin to clearly see where your life is going. It all becomes mapped out, knowwhatImean? Then one day it occurs to you that this *is* your life. So you make changes, try to have a baby, write something that'll never be published, see old friends –.

BEN. Buy a tank with nowhere to park.

MARTHA. Settle! …Sometimes these changes are little wake up calls, other times they're life-changing events.

HANNAH. Martha, I think we already know.

MARTHA. So I've decided, after great forethought to… to… this is so difficult. I don't want it to change our life long friendship.

BEN. Just say it!

HANNAH. It won't change anything, we'll always be friends. Isn't that right dear?

FRANKLYN. *(not so sure)* Oh yeah, friends forever.

MARTHA. Good. Cause I've decided…okay, here goes…I've decided to become…You ready?

BEN. Say it! Just say it!

MARTHA. Settle!

BEN. I'll settle if you say it!

MARTHA. …I've…I've decided to become a Christian–

HANNAH. And that's okay, but first do me a favor and consider a marriage a counselor. I promised Frankie I'd never tell anyone this, but we saw one once–

FRANKLYN. Hannah–

HANNAH. I think it's important that we be honest dear. *(to BEN and MARTHA)* It wasn't easy, because everyone thinks we're the perfect couple, but we did see a counselor for almost two years–

FRANKLYN. Hannah, I–

HANNAH. Then we went to a couples therapy group and a renewal weekend sponsored by our temple.

FRANKLYN. Sweetheart–

HANNAH. They need us—

FRANKLYN. I don't think you heard!

HANNAH. Sure I did, they're getting a divorce.

FRANKLYN. No, she's becoming a Christian.

HANNAH. A what? *(to* **MARTHA***)* A what?

MARTHA. …The other night Ben and I had a fight. What was it about? The S.U.V.? The bills?

BEN. The dogs.

MARTHA. Oh, the dogs, right.

BEN. *(to* **FRANKLYN***)* Never get a lab. Adorable but way dumb. And two is a catastrophe. They, like, feed off each other's dumbness.

MARTHA. My husband was about to walk out, like he always does –.

BEN. I don't *always* walk out.

MARTHA. You *always* walk out!

BEN. Now and then, not *always*.

MARTHA. You disappear for hours and hours.

BEN. To walk the dumb dogs! If I don't, they go insane and attack the slipcovers!

MARTHA. I worry and worry. So I thought no, I'm going to walk out this time. It's my turn to disappear into the night for three and a half hours!

BEN. One hour tops! To get my head together and to save the slipcovers!

MARTHA. I walked and walked. Then I came upon this little funeral parlor. Lights on. People leaving. I walked in. Two funerals. One rather well attended. Family. Children. People sharing hugs. The other – totally empty. I was drawn to the empty one. He was a nice man. Older. But no flowers. No nothing. They were about to put the lights out, then these two acne-faced assistants come in. I asked where are the flowers? They didn't know – and if I didn't mind, could I step back cause they needed to seal the casket so they could go home. And then they bring in this huge welding arc. I kid you not – an industrial strength welding arc. I asked who he was – they didn't care. Did he have family – didn't know. And then one of them fires up the welder. And adjusts the hot, white flame to a whisper. And then they lowered the lid. And I found myself yelling out, "Wait!" And I ran up for one last look at whom ever he was. A kind looking man...someone's lover, husband, daddy. That's when I did it...

BEN. Yes, you did it all right.

MARTHA. I...

HANNAH. Martha what did you do?

MARTHA. I took off my wedding ring and put it in the casket.

HANNAH. You what?

BEN. And they sealed it. Tell'em! Soldered it shut!

MARTHA. ...And they soldered it...

BEN. And then she became a Lutheran!

HANNAH. ...Martha, why?

BEN. There's the sixty four thousand dollar question!

MARTHA. I don't know...It was a sudden thing...I wanted to make a statement.

BEN. A statement! A two and a half karat statement! It was my mother's! Been in the family for years. My grand-mother saved it from the Nazis by shoving it up my grandfather's colon!

(**MARTHA** *breaks down in tears.*)

(*an offstage bing*)

HANNAH. Oh, that's the oven. Martha, come in the kitchen and we'll get you a cup of tea. It'll be all right. (*with a stern look to* **FRANKLYN**) Frankie...

FRANKLYN. (*aside to* **HANNAH**) We can't ask them now.

HANNAH. Just take care of things.

(**HANNAH** *hustles* **MARTHA** *in the kitchen.*)

(*Pause.* **BEN** *and* **FRANKLYN** *just sit there looking at their drinks. Now and then we can hear* **MARTHA** *crying in the kitchen. Finally...*)

FRANKLYN. …So these friends are stuck in the subway and–

BEN. A thousand to choose from and she chooses Lutheran! Explain that one! She even attended a new members potluck. Took knish!

FRANKLYN. Look, Ben, it's obvious you-two are having some problems–

BEN. Want to compare notes?

FRANKLYN. I don't know if I can.

BEN. You gotta come up with something brilliant to save my marriage, something like web flowers Friday.

FRANKLYN. Okay. Ah…You two should talk.

BEN. We've been talking for years.

FRANKLYN. Then perhaps you should consult with your rabbi.

BEN. Oh great advice. Hello Rabbi Liebman, I'd like you to meet my wife Martha Luther. …I knew she was listening to Garrison Keillor a lot, but who knew there were consequences?

FRANKLYN. What happened? Last time we got together you seemed so happy. And Martha was so Jewish – I mean the Cheez-it incident.

BEN. Happy? That's a laugh. Martha and I are one of those couples who fight in public. Admit it. We fight in public.

FRANKLYN. Little love spats, it's nothing,

BEN. Love spats? She and I are always making nasty little comments – always having little schisms in public places. Don't you hate couples who do that? Admit it, it's annoying – say it.

FRANKLYN. Ben–

BEN. Say it.

FRANKLYN. It's a little annoying.

BEN. And Martha and I do it all the time.

FRANKLYN. You do it a lot.

BEN. Now that wasn't hard, was it? You know what I hate are people who hand out advice on marriage when in fact they've been seeing a marriage counselor for two years. That's annoying.

FRANKLYN. Ben –.

BEN. Admit it, that's annoying.

FRANKLYN. That's annoying.

BEN. Well, I'm glad we got that off our chests. How bout them Dodgers.

FRANKLYN. Ben…I think there are other things we need to talk about.

BEN. No we don't.

FRANKLYN. Your marriage is in trouble.

BEN. My marriage is over. Yours is in trouble.

FRANKLYN. Is not.

BEN. Trust me, all marriages are in trouble. Except yours, of course, yours is perfect.

FRANKLYN. I'm sorry that you thought Hannah and I were perfect. We got problems too. Everyday problems –. Life is full of problems.

BEN. So whose fault is it?

FRANKLYN. It's no one's fault – That's life.

BEN. No, whose fault is it that you don't have kids?

FRANKLYN. …Ben, that's too personal.

BEN. So it's your fault.

FRANKLYN. It doesn't matter.

BEN. You shootin' blanks my friend?

FRANKLYN. Ben –.

BEN. I know this doctor –.

FRANKLYN. We saw him. We've been seeing Dr. Rosen for almost two years, okay?…Hannah's ovaries are… underdeveloped. For some reason they never fully matured. She's been taking these drugs – They make her a little sick…nausea, fatigue…We've been told to…hold out little hope.

BEN. …Adoption?

FRANKLYN. You know that's not an option.

BEN. Oh. Right. No. They wouldn't remember. They wouldn't look that deep. What's it been five years?

FRANKLYN. Three and a half.

BEN. Still in a wheelchair?

FRANKLYN. He's progressed to a walker.

BEN. So? It's not the end of the world. Nazi Martians, with strong immune systems, attacking from Mars, that's the end of the world. This is nothing more than a simple pedestrian-Honda incident. You were distracted, Wilshire's hell, it could've happened to anybody.

FRANKLYN. But it happened to me.

BEN. So you ran over your own Rabbi in a crosswalk after temple – He survived.

FRANKLYN. The application form clearly says. "Arrest record." It's right there on the JAA form.

BEN. JAA?

FRANKLYN. Jewish Adoption Agency.

BEN. Does it gotta be Jewish?

FRANKLYN. …You're right…

BEN. I know this guy, he works for an agency in San Diego. He can get you a Ukrainian baby. It's easy, you fly to Kiev and in this back alley you hand this lookout 10,000 Hryvnias and he gives you a baby – All perfectly legal. And you can choose what you want: a socialist or a communist baby.

(**FRANKLYN** *walks away.*)

BEN. What?

FRANKLYN. …And of course being Purim you know what's going to happen.

BEN. No. He doesn't still call does he?

FRANKLYN. Every Purim, a little tipsy, he calls just to let me know that he "bears no grudge." Just as we're sitting down to eat, without fail, the phone rings and he tells me now he's doing fine and that getting hit in that crosswalk was the best thing that ever happened cause it let him slow down and see life with new eyes. And then he'll give me that little speech about how there is no such thing as a coincidence. And all he succeeds in doing is making me feel like crap.

BEN. You were lucky, God looked out for you.

FRANKLYN. No, Hannah's father looked out for me…You know it pays to marry the daughter of one of L.A.'s top attorneys. I just wish he could've paid off the L.A.P.D.

BEN. You know what you two are, Hannah and you, you're macaroni. It's true. You two are macaroni and cheese. You belong together. Martha and I, on the other hand, we're pickles and mustard – we make no sense.

FRANKLYN. I just never understood your marriage, not wanting children – What type of marriage is that? We want family and we can't. You don't want and you can. That, my friend, that's annoying.

BEN. What about….donation. You find some one who'll donate some eggs, you know what I mean, embryos not omelets, problem solved.

FRANKLYN. As a matter of fact, tonight, before you announced you were getting a divorce, that's exactly what we were going to ask.

BEN. You wanted Martha's eggs – wow, you are desperate.

FRANKLYN. But then I was going to go one step further. …I was going to ask you to… Make a donation… Also.

BEN. …Me? Why me?

FRANKLYN. When we found the problem with Hannah, we didn't look any further, but then I went to a doctor and found…

BEN. You *are* shooting blanks, I knew it! I always knew you were a low sperm count kinda fella –.

FRANKLYN. …I haven't told Hannah.

BEN. Wait a minute –. That means that you-two would have us-two's baby?

FRANKLYN. Correct.

BEN. Wow, that's sick. Really really sick.

FRANKLYN. ...I just don't get it. ...You'd think that someone who's harmed a life should be allowed to make up
for it. And your divorce is the topper. It's almost as if
God has it out for us...

BEN. You know, Martha is always saying, why can't we be
more like Frankie and Hannah. More like macaroni
and cheese. But you two are more screwed up than us
whom everyone thinks is screwed up. And now you've
taken a leap off the deep end my friend.

FRANKLYN. How's that?

BEN. Writing a novel? That's the surest way to destroy a
marriage. All these other curveballs – no children,
quitting your job, running down your own Rabbi on
Wilshire Boulevard – all of that a marriage can endure,
but writing a novel? Your relationship is farkakta.

FRANKLYN. I've screwed it up even more than that.

BEN. How could you screw it up more than that?

FRANKLYN. ...I've met someone.

BEN. ...What?

FRANKLYN. A night school professor –.

BEN. Hold on.

FRANKLYN. I haven't done anything –.

BEN. I said hold on!

(He makes sure the hallway is empty.)

BEN. What the hell are you saying?

FRANKLYN. Maybe Hannah and my relationship is just bad
luck, maybe it wasn't meant to be.

BEN. So you're having an affair?

FRANKLYN. No. We just talk. But it's clear, if I'm interested,
she's interested. We...talk...

BEN. Talk – about what?

FRANKLYN. Things... Her car was in the shop. She needed
a lift home after class. So we...talked. Then this week
it was in the shop again, I think on purpose, so I had
to pick her up. And then after reading my opening

scene in class she said it made her hungry so we went out for a late night…snack. If Hannah asks, I told her I was with you.

BEN. So you're lying to your very own wife.

FRANKLYN. Not lying, I just haven't told her.

BEN. You know Martha and I may fight in public but we don't lie. If her hair looks like some sort of hideous hellhole I'm honest about it. If I got day-old broccoli stuck between my bicuspids, she lets me know. But we don't lie. And the perfect couple shouldn't either –.

FRANKLYN. Where does this perfect couple crap come from?

BEN. You're the perfect couple.

FRANKLYN. Says who?

BEN. Everyone. My parents, your parents. Her parents. Rabbi Marks. Rabbi Greenberg –.

FRANKLYN. Well we're not! *(beat)* Martha's right, there comes a point when your life seems all plotted out for you. And sometimes the only answer is to shake things up.

BEN. With a night school professor? This isn't like you.

FRANKLYN. Why not?

BEN. Frankie, no matter how you cook it, you can't dress up macaroni, it'll always be macaroni.

FRANKLYN. …The other night, Hannah went to her hairdresser, like she does the first of every month for seven years now – same hairdresser – Seven years. And she's gone for one hour and twenty minutes. Without fail – One hour and twenty minutes. Like clockwork.

BEN. And that's when you call Miss Night School Professor.

FRANKLYN. Thought about it, but no. I just sit here. And then I look at the clock and it occurs to me that she's been gone for two hours. Then two hours and ten minutes so I begin to worry –.

BEN. Ahah! She knows about your indiscretion and so she's having a revenge fling with her hunky hairdresser.

FRANKLYN. Hannah's not the type.

BEN. Nor are you my friend.

FRANKLYN. ...So I call her cell phone. It rings in the bedroom. She forgot it again – She's always forgetting her cell phone. So, I decide to call the salon. You know, just to make sure everything's okay. So I go to look up Hairdresser Haven, but the phone book is missing – Hannah's always losing the phone book. So I think maybe I'll go over –.

BEN. To catch her red handed with her hunky hairdresser.

FRANKLYN. I open the front door and I come face to face –.

BEN. With!

FRANKLYN. This kid. I jump. He jumps. By coincidence he just happens to be delivering the new phone book – A total fluke. He hands it over and walks off. So, I'm looking up the number and then I see it – The last thing I expected. Right there in the white pages. I see...The word, "Happiness."

BEN. Happiness?

FRANKLYN. Right there. In-between "Dale and Jean Happart" and "Hardwood flooring of Van Nuys." And beside it this number.

BEN. "Happiness," like all by itself?

FRANKLYN. All by itself.

BEN. And a number?

FRANKLYN. 818 area code.

BEN. Really? Happiness is right here in the Valley. Who would've guessed. You called?

FRANKLYN. Thought about it. But...What if it's a porn line? Or drugs? It could be anything. So I...I ripped the page out of the book – Been carrying it around for a week.

BEN. Wow man, that's really...really... Sick.

FRANKLYN. Wanta call?

BEN. No – It's probably a porn line. ...Look, I'm going to give you advice. I know, I know, it's usually the other way around. More like, always the other way around, but I'm going to do it. For the first time in our friendship I'm giving you some advice.

FRANKLYN. Okay.

(beat)

BEN. Have you considered becoming Lutheran?

FRANKLYN. Would you be serious.

BEN. What? Frankie, it's not the end of the world. Hermann Goering returning to earth with fission powered laser beams for eyes – That's the end of the world. This is nothing but a blip. You got it made. You found a sweet grade school teacher with zero temper who'll stick to you like glue. You cripple a Rabbi and he forgives you. You get married and her father is rich. You can't have children so you'll adopt a socialist baby. Frankie, the only person who can ruin your life is you. That's not the case with most of us schmucks. So when are you going to stop and see that you're one of the lucky ones.

FRANKLYN. Then how come I feel so unlucky?

(HANNAH and MARTHA enter. Both are crying big fat tears of joy. It takes them a moment to pull themselves together.)

BEN. What?

HANNAH. We have an announcement.

FRANKLYN. Oh god no.

HANNAH. You wanta do it or should I?

MARTHA. You – You're better at announcements.

HANNAH. Okay. Martha has agreed…

(They laugh and hug. More tears.)

BEN. What?! Say it!

MARTHA. Shut up and be happy for her!

BEN. Be happy for what?!

MARTHA. Shut up and she'll tell you!

BEN. Tell me what? What the hell is going on?

MARTHA. Settle!

HANNAH. …Martha has agreed to… *(more crying)*

BEN. What?!

MARTHA. SETTLE!

HANNAH. Eggs! Martha agreed to donate her eggs – Isn't that wonderful? We were talking and I knew it wasn't the right time and I suddenly found myself blurting out the question and she said yes.

FRANKLYN. You okay with this?

MARTHA. I think it's wonderful. I think it makes a statement!

FRANKLYN. But I thought you hated needles.

HANNAH. It's not that bad. She'll have to take fertility drugs and then the doctors will harvest them with a small needle – Aren't you happy?

FRANKLYN. Sure.

HANNAH. Dr. Rosen did say it was our only hope. And using Martha's eggs will keep it in the family. Besides, it's not the type of question you ask common friends. You gotta know someone, someone you can trust, someone who won't tell my grandparents.

MARTHA. You know I went to Dr. Rosen this afternoon. It should've hit me then. It's such an obvious answer.

BEN. So let me get this straight. You'd be the mother, but you'd be the…mother.

MARTHA. No, I'd be the egg donor. *(to **HANNAH**)* Although I'd prefer to be called Aunt. Is that okay?

BEN. Aunt Egg Donor?

HANNAH. I think it's wonderful. Am I right, Honey?

FRANKLYN. *(not so thrilled)* Yes. Martha is having my child – This calls for a drink.

*(**FRANKLYN** pours himself a large glass of wine and chugs it.)*

HANNAH. I kept thinking, it's not the right time and then suddenly I just sorta blurted it out.

MARTHA. We're family, it's okay to blurt.

HANNAH. But I mean with, you know, the divorce and everything, it just wasn't the right time. But I guess sometimes you just gotta go with your gut feeling.

MARTHA. That's the second time you've mentioned divorce, what divorce?

HANNAH. Oh Martha, you don't have to hide it, Ben told us.

MARTHA. …Told you what? You told'em we were getting a divorce?

BEN. I asked you not to tell.

MARTHA. And when were you going to tell me!

BEN. I was going to tell you.

MARTHA. When?!

BEN. I was goin' to say it!

MARTHA. But when?!

BEN. …Right now. I'm telling you right now! I want a divorce!

MARTHA. Oh my god. And you told them, these two people, first? What type of sick thing is that?

HANNAH. I'm so sorry, Martha, I thought you knew.

MARTHA. Oh my god…I'm so humiliated. You! You are a shit head. And you too!

FRANKLYN. What did I do?

MARTHA. You encouraged him.

FRANKLYN. We compared notes.

MARTHA. Is he having an affair?

FRANKLYN. What?

MARTHA. He told you everything else. Is he having an affair?

(**BEN** and **FRANKLYN** don't have an answer.)

MARTHA. I heard you-two talking! Just now, I went to get a tissue. I went down the hall to the bathroom and I heard you two talking about my husband having an affair! I could barely hear but I could tell. An affair with a night school professor. Admit it Ben, admit it!

(HANNAH looks at FRANKLYN, he doesn't cover well.)

BEN. I don't know what you're talking about.

MARTHA. Where would a man like you meet a night school professor. And why a professor would have anything to do with The Big and Tall Clothing King of L.A. is a mystery to me, but I heard!

BEN. Why would I have an affair I'm so happily married!

MARTHA. You want a divorce, you gotta divorce! But I'm taking the house!

BEN. You're not taking the house!

MARTHA. I'm taking the house and the gym membership!

BEN. Go ahead, take the gym membership; maybe for once you'll use it!

MARTHA. And I'm changing the locks and you'll never see your XR68 again!

BEN. My what?!

MARTHA. Your Weber grill!

BEN. You wouldn't!

HANNAH. Everyone Shut Up! Just Shut Up! SETTLE!

(Her uncharacteristic outburst silences them. Pause.)

HANNAH. *(pulling herself together)* Dinner is ready! Can we please just gather at the table. And keep our mouths – sealed!

(HANNAH plants herself at the table. No one joins her. Pause. BEN grabs his jacket.)

MARTHA. You're walking out?

BEN. I'm not walking out, I'm going for a walk – And Frankie's comin' with.

FRANKLYN. Huh?

BEN. We're going for a walk to get our heads together so we can come back and not ruin the evening!

MARTHA. Going for a walk. That makes so much sense! So logical!

BEN. Logical? *You* want logical?! Okay. Hey Franklyn, I got a great idea, saw a cemetery around the corner – let's go find an open grave and bury our wallets!

(**BEN** *exits.*)

FRANKLYN. We'll…be right back.

(**FRANKLYN** *exits.* **HANNAH** *sits alone at the table.* **MARTHA** *joins her. Pause. After several moments* **MARTHA** *tries a little small talk.*)

MARTHA. So what're you teaching?

HANNAH. What?

MARTHA. Arithmetic, I'll bet you're teaching the kids arithmetic.

HANNAH. Ah. No. Grammar.

MARTHA. Oh. Like verbs and nouns?

HANNAH. Martha…

MARTHA. No, you don't have to ask. Just so you won't worry, the whole egg thing is still a go.

HANNAH. I'm so sorry. I didn't know you didn't know.

MARTHA. Obviously, there's a lot I don't know. My marriage? It's a laugh. Ben and I are one of those couples who fight in public. Have you noticed that?

HANNAH. No, I've never noticed.

MARTHA. We both know you're lying. Admit it. You're lying.

HANNAH. I'm lying.

MARTHA. See that wasn't that hard. (*beat*) So you're covering nouns.

HANNAH. And verbs.

MARTHA. You gotta give it a nice noun.

HANNAH. It?

MARTHA. The baby. How about Zoe, it means "life."

HANNAH. I haven't let myself think that far ahead yet.

MARTHA. How 'bout Shana Boshsa – It means beautiful daughter of God. That's a nice name. But whatever you do, I beg you, don't name it Martha. Not a Jewish name…It's a loser's name…

(**MARTHA** *holds back tears.*)

HANNAH. Oh, Martha…

MARTHA. ...When my sister lost Isaac, I resolved that I wouldn't allow God to put me through that. ...I was there that morning. Was babysitting so that they could finally have a weekend together alone...that wonderful little boy – sleeping so soundly – only he wasn't asleep. ...And everything that followed. I promised, I promised myself right then and there that I'd never allow God to hurt me like he hurt my sister.

(Beat, MARTHA *has a drink.)*

HANNAH. And so Lutheranism is the answer?

MARTHA. Why not?

HANNAH. Don't you think it's kind of a major leap? Perhaps you should start with, like, Jews for Jesus and then sorta work your way to Martin Luther.

MARTHA. ...Have you ever noticed that everyone you know, without exception, doesn't get what they need. My mother, a good woman, dies when I'm twelve. Ben's mother, I'm not saying anything you can't already vouch for, she's a jerk, and healthy as a horse. Ben's father, a kind man, we should all have such a caring soul in our lives, gone in an instant. My father who won't put on pants to answer the door, alive and kicking. My sister...No, we won't go there again... *(beat)* At first I thought that God had left the receiver off the hook. Then I concluded, after much thought and evidence, that God doesn't micromanage...But now, now I'm convinced, God isn't even a noun.

*(*MARTHA *can't hold the tears back any longer.)*

HANNAH. ...It's Purim. We're supposed to celebrate the inexplicable coincidences that shape our lives. Don't you believe that these coincidences are really evidence of something operating behind the scenes?

MARTHA. No Hannah, there are no coincidences, only curveballs that some of us mistake for coincidences.

HANNAH. Martha...

MARTHA. All my friends talk about the permanent uncertainty of life – the phone rings and suddenly your life is thrown into chaos. Yet, for me, everything is clear. And so I've decided I'm going to start throwing a few curveballs of my own. Lutheran – make a bet God never saw that one coming.

HANNAH. You can make your marriage work.

(**MARTHA** *laughs through her tears.*)

MARTHA. Do you know what my husband is doing right now?

HANNAH. ...walking?

MARTHA. He's out there measuring the parking spot!

HANNAH. No.

MARTHA. Ten to one. Ten to one, he's out measuring.

HANNAH. Where would he find a measuring tape?

MARTHA. He's the Big and Tall King of L.A., he buys measuring tapes of every shape and size by the gross.

HANNAH. Why would he do such a thing?

MARTHA. To prove me wrong. But I don't care. He can go parking with his night school professor.

HANNAH. What did they say about a night school professor?

MARTHA. It was muffled, but I could hear them talking about a late night dinner.

HANNAH. But you're sure it was night school?

MARTHA. That's what I heard. ...So we will divorce, Ben'll have his fling. I'm not telling you anything you don't already know, trust me, it'll end badly. Once she has an in-depth conversation with him she'll realize that the Big and Tall King of L.A. has a small and tiny... mind. They'll break up. He'll beg for forgiveness, but I'll say I'm too busy with doctor Rosen. We'll get you your baby. Your marriage will flourish. And then maybe many years from now we'll meet at a family reunion. But when we do, promise me you won't show me your precious child...for the child will only remind me of Ben...

HANNAH. Then I won't do it.

MARTHA. Yes you will – cause we're going to throw God a curveball. We're going to show him that we can create our own coincidences. L'chai-im.

(**MARTHA** *takes a drink.* **BEN** *walks in followed by* **FRANKLYN**.)

BEN. I have proof!

(**BEN** *pulls out a large measuring tape.*)

BEN. Frankie, if you will assist me.

FRANKLYN. Ben, I don't think this is a good idea.

BEN. I have spatial intelligence! Take the other end.

(**FRANKLYN** *takes one end of the measuring tape.* **BEN** *pulls it out.*)

BEN. This is the length of your Cadillac EXT – 222.4 inches. Franklyn would you kindly mark 222.4 inches.

(**FRANKLYN** *reluctantly marks 222.4 inches.*)

BEN. And here is the length of my BMW – 192 inches please.

(**FRANKLYN** *reluctantly marks 192 inches.*)

BEN. And here is the length of the parking spot you *assumed* I took from you. Frankie?

FRANKLYN. Ben, I really –.–

BEN. No. When I'm right I'm right. Please!

(**FRANKLYN** *marks a place on the tape.*)

BEN. And how many inches is that?

FRANKLYN. 219.5 inches.

BEN. And how long is her Cadillac EXT.

FRANKLYN. 222.4 inches.

BEN. Difference of?

FRANKLYN. 2.9 inches.

BEN. I rest my case. We can eat!

(**BEN** *walks over and plants himself at the table. Beat.*)

MARTHA. We can eat.

HANNAH. Why not.

(*They reluctantly gather at the table.*)

FRANKLYN. Haven't we forgotten something?

HANNAH. Oh, that's right – food.

(*The phone rings. Beat.*)

HANNAH. Sweetheart, that's for you.

FRANKLYN. Would you tell Rabbi Marks that we are about to eat.

HANNAH. (*bitter*) No, I think you should answer it.

FRANKLYN. (*throwing down his napkin*) …Fine. (*pissed, to* **BEN** *and* **MARTHA**) This will only take only a second, he's just gotta tell me how absolutely wonderful life is since I took his legs from him!

(**FRANKLYN** *grudgingly answers the phone.*)

FRANKLYN. (*on phone*) Hello…Oh hello. So sorry, I didn't expect you to call…Dr. Rosen.

(**HANNAH** *stiffens.*)

FRANKLYN. (*on phone*) Yes. She's right here.

(**HANNAH** *moves towards the phone.*)

FRANKLYN. No. It's for you, Martha.

HANNAH. What?

FRANKLYN. It's Dr. Rosen. He wants to talk to you.

MARTHA. Me? Why me?

FRANKLYN. Don't know.

(**MARTHA** *takes the phone.*)

MARTHA. (*on phone*) Hello?…Well, hello Dr. Rosen…No, we were just sitting down to eat…I'm so sorry I must've turned my cell phone off…Yes, I did mention that I was coming over here for Purim…Oh, yes we're having a lovely evening, just family, friends and good conversation…What? …Oh…If it's okay I'd rather take the news standing up. (*pause, she listens.*) …I understand. …Yes…Thank you for calling…

(**MARTHA** *slowly hangs up.*)

MARTHA. *(to* **BEN***)* How's this for a curveball sweetheart? You're going to be a daddy.

(**BEN***'s knees weaken. He sits.*)

(*blackout*)

End of Act One

ACT TWO
Scene One

Hanukah

(The lights rise on **ALISON** *an innocent eighteen-year-old girl who is eight months pregnant. She reads* **FRANK-LYN***'s "novelette" manuscript and eats a pickle. She finishes the pickle, stretches and rubs her very expectant stomach.)*

ALISON. More pickles please!

*(***FRANKLYN*** enters.)*

FRANKLYN. Did I hear someone say they want another pickle?

ALISON. Yeah, I like the big ones.

FRANKLYN. With whipped cream or mustard this time?

ALISON. The works.

FRANKLYN. You got it. One big pickle with whipped cream and mustard dipped in nuts coming up.

(He starts for the kitchen/hall – stops.)

FRANKLYN. *(indicating his novel manuscript)* Oh by the way, what do you think so far?

ALISON. Oh, it's good.

FRANKLYN. You know Hannah, she never really liked the idea of me writing a novel.

ALISON. Really.

FRANKLYN. Thought it was a waste of time. But nine months later how things have changed.

ALISON. I really like it…so far.

FRANKLYN. Not that I'm fishing for compliments, but what do you like?

ALISON. You mean like specifics?

FRANKLYN. I'm open to notes.

ALISON. Well, let's see…I really have to say that I like the font you're using.

FRANKLYN. …That's what you like about my novel – the font?

ALISON. Yeah, it's really easy on the eyes.

FRANKLYN. What about story? Character?

ALISON. Oh that…Yeah, that's nice too. Not as good as the font.

FRANKLYN. What about the subway scene where Joey is accidentally electrocuted by the third rail?

ALISON. That's okay.

FRANKLYN. Only okay?

ALISON. Sure – What's a third rail?

FRANKLYN. I take it you've never been to New York.

ALISON. New York City? No. And they don't have subways in Iowa. I do have one note, if you're interested.

FRANKLYN. Sure.

ALISON. The first scene –.

FRANKLYN. The dinner party scene?

ALISON. It's kinda predictable. I mean, all they do is talk. Who wants to read a novel with a bunch of people talking and eating? All it did was make me hungry.

FRANKLYN. For pickles.

ALISON. Dipped in nuts.

FRANKLYN. Coming right up.

ALISON. Would you mind if I did a little editing?

FRANKLYN. You mean like in the text?

ALISON. If you want help.

FRANKLYN. *(reluctant)* …Sure. If you find a sentence or two that you think is…predictable…feel free to put a little light check mark by it.

ALISON. Will do. Thanks for my pickle.

FRANKLYN. With whipped cream, mustard and –.

FRANKLYN & ALISON. Nuts.

(*FRANKLYN exits to the hallway/kitchen.* **ALISON** *reads, she stops and crosses out a sentence. Then reads more. She crosses out a paragraph. Reads more and crosses out a page. And the next page.*)

(**HANNAH** *enters with groceries.*)

HANNAH. Hi, Honey, I'm home – ! Alison!

ALISON. Hi Hannah. Is it okay if I call you Hannah?

HANNAH. Sure. That's the way I prefer it –. What are you doing here?

ALISON. Reading Franklyn's novel.

HANNAH. And, ah, how's that going for you?

ALISON. (*crossing out another page*) Doing a little editing.

HANNAH. Where's my husband?

ALISON. (*crossing out another page*) In the kitchen.

HANNAH. Let me guess, with his head in the oven?

ALISON. No, he's getting me a pickle. I've also made a decision about my baby.

HANNAH. Really? That's wonderful. Let me get him –.

(**FRANKLYN** *enters with a pickle covered in whipped cream, mustard and nuts.*)

FRANKLYN. Here we go. One pickle dipped in – hi dear.

HANNAH. Hi.

(*They exchange a nervous kiss. The following is done with forced kindness but growing to obvious anger.*)

HANNAH. Alison says that she's made a decision.

FRANKLYN. Yes I know. I tried to call but you forgot your cell phone...again.

HANNAH. I know, I tried to call to say that I was stuck in traffic.

FRANKLYN. But you didn't.

HANNAH. That's because I didn't have my phone.

FRANKLYN. One shouldn't forget one's cell phone cause one never knows who might unexpectedly drop in out of the blue and change everything.

HANNAH. Yes, I won't make that mistake again!

FRANKLYN. Good, cause one shouldn't forget should one?

HANNAH. I've made a note of it!

FRANKLYN. I just want to make the point!

HANNAH. The point's been made – !

ALISON. Are you fighting?

HANNAH. *(big smile)* …What? Oh, no, we don't fight.

FRANKLYN. As a matter of fact our best friends, Ben and Martha, they call us macaroni and cheese cause we never fight, do we dear?

HANNAH. Never.

FRANKLYN. Ever.

HANNAH. Kisses?

FRANKLYN. Yes, kisses.

(They give each other a quick peck.)

FRANKLYN. Hey, they're supposed to be here any moment. You can ask them yourself – they'll confirm it – We're the perfect couple.

*(**FRANKLYN** hands the pickle to **ALISON**.)*

ALISON. Good, cause my parents, all they do is fight – All the time I was growing up. I think it affects children when grownups fight.

HANNAH. We couldn't agree more, could we dear?

FRANKLYN. Fighting – terrible.

ALISON. And they'd fight even more if they knew I was pregnant.

FRANKLYN. Well, they're never going to find out.

ALISON. Good. Cause there'd be hell to pay.

HANNAH. …So, Alison, you've thought about our offer?

ALISON. Yes. I'm sorry it took so long.

HANNAH. Oh, not at all. We thought it'd take about three and a half weeks, didn't we dear?

FRANKLYN. Longer even – not that longer is good.

HANNAH. Right, one should be decisive in cases like this.

FRANKLYN. For the child.

HANNAH. Right, for the child.

ALISON. That's what I've been thinking – and you seem like such a nice couple.

HANNAH. We are.

FRANKLYN. And we never fight.

ALISON. Last night I was trying to figure out what I was going to tell my parents about not coming home for the holidays. If they found out, they'd kill me. I swear they'd kill me so fast. They still think I'm in diapers.

HANNAH. Well, sometimes we all make mistakes. But it's possible to make things right, isn't it dear?

FRANKLYN. Oh yeah, mistakes, I've made tons of mistakes but I always make them right.

ALISON. I'm uncomfortable lying to them. But I guess sometimes life gets so complicated that you just haveta not think about yourself.

HANNAH. I never think about myself.

FRANKLYN. And I think of myself even less then she does.

ALISON. So, if you got that contract. I'll sign.

(HANNAH and FRANKLYN desperately try to contain their joy.)

FRANKLYN. *(giddy)* Well, I do just happen to have it right here. *(to HANNAH)* Where do I have it?

HANNAH. In the study.

FRANKLYN. The study?

HANNAH. Yes, the study, dear.

FRANKLYN. What study?

HANNAH. The room with the desk.

FRANKLYN. Right. The study.

(FRANKLYN runs out.)

(Beat, HANNAH and ALISON sit for a moment – They are at a loss for words.)

HANNAH. I just want you to know that you're making the right decision. Your baby will be loved and never want...

ALISON. Cool.

(Beat. ALISON eats her pickle. HANNAH grabs a pen and scribbles on a piece of paper.)

HANNAH. *(nervous)* Let's see – is it working? Oh, yes the pen is working. Everything's ready.

(an uneasy pause)

ALISON. *(off the menorah)* I like your candle.

HANNAH. Thank you. It was a gift from Bubbe.

ALISON. Bubbe?

HANNAH. My grandmother.

ALISON. Oh, I nearly forgot. I brought you a gift too.

(ALISON reaches into her backpack and pulls out a small stuffed Santa Claus.)

ALISON. I'm so sorry; I didn't have time to wrap it.

HANNAH. Well...That's awfully nice.

ALISON. I was wandering around campus town, saw it, thought you'd like it.

HANNAH. It's...great.

ALISON. One of the reasons I decided to sign the contract is because you seem so much like my family. Except that you don't fight.

HANNAH. Never.

(another uncomfortable pause)

ALISON. ...The only time my parents don't fight is on Christmas Eve...My father won't allow a Christmas tree until Christmas Eve. Then we all get into his pickup and drive to this place where they let you cut down your own tree. Normally there aren't many left but Dad knows the owner and he always saves one perfect tree for us. So we cut it down and my Dad always yells "timber" even though it's only like eight feet tall. And we take it back to the house. And then we drink hot cider and eggnog and the next morning Santa Claus comes – my Dad loves to play Santa Claus, even owns his own suit. He used to rent it but he says owning is cheaper…Is that how you do it?

(**HANNAH** *sits there rather stunned.*)

HANNAH. Well…not exactly.

ALISON. Cause you know, most people have their Christmas trees up by now…Is something wrong?

HANNAH. Ah…No…We should hurry cause friends of ours are coming over tonight.

ALISON. To drink eggnog?

HANNAH. …Sure…Frankie!

FRANKLYN. *(offstage)* Coming!

HANNAH. You know Alison, I was thinking that coming from Iowa – Where in Iowa?

ALISON. Luana.

HANNAH. Small town?

ALISON. Not that small – One hundred and ninety.

HANNAH. I see. Coming from Luana, being in L.A. must be quite a shock.

ALISON. Sure is.

HANNAH. Do they have much cultural diversity in Luana?

ALISON. Oh sure, my high school had a whole day devoted to cultural diversity.

HANNAH. A whole day – Imagine that.

ALISON. We studied how Christmas is celebrated around the world. Did you know that in Russia on Christmas Eve they eat a porridge called kutya?

HANNAH. Didn't know that.

ALISON. I try to learn something every day.

HANNAH. Me too…Did you know that Los Angeles has the largest Jewish population of any city in the United States?

ALISON. If you say so.

HANNAH. I was reading the other day that only 28 percent of Americans know someone who is Muslim. Only 17 percent know a Hindu or Buddhist, but a full 51 percent say they know someone who's Jewish.

ALISON. Oh.

HANNAH. Do you know anyone Jewish?

ALISON. I guess I'm one of the 49 percent. I did see a Woody Allen movie once – didn't get it.

HANNAH. So you don't know much about Jews.

ALISON. There was this Jewish girl in my high school once – She didn't stay long. Seemed out of place so I thought I'd make her happy. I found out it was something called "Yom Kipper."

HANNAH. Yom Kipp*ur.*

ALISON. So I went out of my way to wish her a Happy Yom Kippur. Even went to the Hallmark Card store over in Waterloo and tried to find a Merry Yom Kippur card but they were out.

HANNAH. So you've never really known any Jews.

ALISON. All I know about them is what my Dad told me.

HANNAH. Which is?

ALISON. He said they're nice people.

HANNAH. Good.

ALISON. And that they have a lot of traditions.

HANNAH. True, many beautiful traditions.

ALISON. He also said there was this special thing they like to read…Has a "T" in it.

HANNAH. The Torah?

ALISON. No.

HANNAH. The Talmud?

ALISON. No. The New York Times…He also said that Arabs got problems with'em…Oh, there was something else he said…What was it? Oh that's right – They control Hollywood and they killed Jesus.

(**FRANKLYN** *enters with the contract.*)

FRANKLYN. Found it! And a pen – that works. Alison, I want you to know that this contract has been written up by Levy, Levy and Goldstein, one of the best law firms in L.A.

ALISON. I have no doubt, Dad says Jews really make good lawyers.

HANNAH. Frankie –.

FRANKLYN. *(not listening)* As you can see, all your medical costs will be paid as well as your tuition at Cal State Northridge for the next three years – or any other *state* college you wish to transfer to –

HANNAH. Sweetheart – !

FRANKLYN. In a minute, dear – Oh! This I think you'll like – the new contract includes an addendum that states that you'll receive a brand new Mini Cooper convertible, or equivalent automobile – paid for by Levy, Levy and Goldstein –

HANNAH. Frankie!

FRANKLYN. So if you'll just put your old John Hancock right here, here and here and initial here, here and there we'll be in business –

HANNAH. Alison, would you like another pickle?

ALISON. Thanks but I've had six.

HANNAH. I think you need another.

ALISON. I'm sorta full.

HANNAH. How about if you go the kitchen, help yourself to anything and study the contract.

FRANKLYN. But we can do that right here dear –

HANNAH. I want Alison to have a pickle –.

FRANKLYN. But she hasn't finished the pickle she's got –.

HANNAH. I want her to have another – !

FRANKLYN. Why would she want another pickle when she hasn't finished this pickle – ?!

HANNAH. Cause I want her to have another – !

ALISON. Are you two fighting?

HANNAH. …No. We don't fight.

FRANKLYN. Never.

HANNAH. Ever. *(double sweet)* Sweetheart, I just thought Alison would like a little time without us hanging over her to study the contract – Okay?

(She elbows him.)

FRANKLYN. Sure.

HANNAH. You'll find a whole big jar of pickles in the back of the fridge. Or...whatever.

ALISON. Okay.

*(**ALISON** takes the contract and exits. Smiling, **FRANKLYN** and **HANNAH** wait for her to exit. Then...)*

FRANKLYN. What?!

HANNAH. She doesn't know we're Jewish!

FRANKLYN. Course she does.

HANNAH. *(holding up the Santa Claus)* She brought us a Christmas present and asked where our Christmas tree was!

FRANKLYN. That's not possible. When we met the first time, I clearly stated that we were Jewish. I made it abundantly clear.

HANNAH. How? How did you make it clear?!

FRANKLYN. I...I...offered her a bagel.

HANNAH. That's it?!

FRANKLYN. Then when we went to dinner we ordered Chinese – Wait, how could she not know we are Jewish, our last names are sort of a give away.

HANNAH. I don't think she knows any Jews. She called our menorah a candle.

FRANKLYN. Oh come on she's seen a menorah before.

HANNAH. She's from Iowa!

FRANKLYN. So?

HANNAH. There are no Jews in Iowa!

FRANKLYN. So what? She'll sign the contract, in a month she drops the kid and drives back to Des Moines in a brand new Mini Cooper. It's a win win situation.

HANNAH. We can't adopt her baby if she doesn't know.

FRANKLYN. Why not?

HANNAH. Cause it wouldn't be right.

FRANKLYN. Hannah, she's agreed to sign! We've been sweating this for three and a half weeks and five years before that!

HANNAH. I can't do it. I can't unless she knows.

FRANKLYN. You're willing to let it all go? Years of fertility treatments, years of nausea and fatigue and so much sex that it isn't even fun anymore. All of that you're willing to sacrifice on a technicality?

HANNAH. Her father told her that Jews control Hollywood and killed Jesus!

FRANKLYN. Killed Jesus? Who the hell is her father Mel Gibson?

(Doorbell. They freeze.)

HANNAH. Who's that?

FRANKLYN. Oh crap, that's right it's Ben and Martha.

HANNAH. What are they doing here?

FRANKLYN. They said they'd stop by – it's Hanukkah. Okay, we can make this work. We just have to make sure that they don't tell Alison it's Hanukkah.

HANNAH. How do we do that?

FRANKLYN. We'll have Hanukkah we just won't mention Hanukkah. We'll say a code word instead. That's it! Every time we'd normally say Hanukkah, we say a code word.

HANNAH. What code word?

FRANKLYN. The code word is…Christmas.

(doorbell)

HANNAH. I won't do it.

FRANKLYN. You will do it, because in a month you'll be holding a wonderful baby.

HANNAH. I will not lie to get a baby.

FRANKLYN. All right! Fine! We'll remain childless. Is that what you want? More of the same? Because that's what's going to happen! More looks. More sympathy and tons of free advice from relatives. Is that what you want?

HANNAH. No! I want my husband to stop seeing a night school professor!

(Beat. Two doorbells.)

FRANKLYN. I dropped that class; you know I dropped it.

HANNAH. Was she pretty?

FRANKLYN. Why are you bringing this up now?

HANNAH. Why did you drop the class? Cause you knew I found out?

FRANKLYN. *(yelling)* Because it wasn't what I wanted!

HANNAH. And what do you want?!

FRANKLYN. I want a family! I want you and this Iowa baby! And I want to raise it to be a good Jew – *(hiding the menorah under the couch)* A proud Jew – Oh crap that's right, the Mezuzah! Gotta get rid of the Mezuzah!

(FRANKLYN runs to the door and tries to pull the mezuzah off the frame.)

HANNAH. Frankie no!

FRANKLYN. It won't budge. Some idiot glued it to the door!

(The door pops open sending FRANKLYN to the floor. It's BEN.)

BEN. What? Are we not answering doorbells today?

HANNAH. Oh, hi, Ben!

BEN. What's this! He's on the floor? Why is he on the floor?

HANNAH. He was just getting the door and –

BEN. Happy Hanukkah big fella!

(BEN helps FRANKLYN to his feet.)

FRANKLYN. Ben.

BEN. Franklyn!

(BEN hugs FRANKLYN.)

BEN. You're not going to believe this! Wonder of wonders! We found a parking spot right out front! Step back. Are you ready? I present to you the queen of all she sees. The most magnificent woman in the world. Lady Martha of Prego!

(BEN holds the door. MARTHA enters – She's nine months pregnant and ready to pop.)

HANNAH. Oh my god!

MARTHA. A week overdue, don't hug me too hard or I might drop it right here!

BEN. Dr. Rosen says he's going to induce labor tomorrow morning. Says the baby's huge. A linebacker. Going to be six foot five at least.

MARTHA. Perfect for running a chain of big and tall shops.

(They help MARTHA to the couch.)

BEN. And we bought a new car. Gas/Electric. 55 miles to the gallon. It's got dual temperature controls – life is too short to live without dual temperature.

(BEN and MARTHA touch noses.)

BEN. Do you love your dual temperature controls?

MARTHA. I love my dual temperature controls.

BEN. Give Daddy a kiss.

BEN & MARTHA. Yum yum yum.

(They kiss like teenagers. HANNAH and FRANKLYN are amazed.)

FRANKLYN. You're…getting along.

BEN. You noticed.

MARTHA. And it's all because of you.

HANNAH. Us?

MARTHA. And that awful night. When was it?

BEN. Purim.

MARTHA. How did you put up with us? Always fighting. Always at each other's throats.

BEN. But that night changed everything. That's why we had to stop in. To thank you, the perfect couple, for saving our marriage.

HANNAH. I don't think we –.

BEN. Yes you did. You suggested that we see a marriage counselor, couples therapy group and the renewal weekend and it worked!

MARTHA. Tomorrow our lives will change forever and I want you to know that it's all because of you.

BEN. Show'em what's on your hand.

(MARTHA *shows off her huge diamond ring.*)

BEN. Do you realize how much it costs to exhume a body? It isn't cheap. And the look on the family's face when we told them why we wanted to do it – Priceless.

MARTHA. It turns out he did have a family. A really nice understanding family who thought we were a bit wacko but gave permission.

BEN. And three thousand dollars and six city permits later – It's back.

MARTHA. And so are my beliefs. Although I've noticed that after being Lutheran for a while, I do use a lot more cream of mushroom soup when I cook.

BEN. You should see the innovative things she can do with Jello!

FRANKLYN. That's interesting that you should bring this up cause we have a big favor to ask.

BEN. Ah! The donation. We talked about it – As soon as this is over we're on. Right dear?

MARTHA. Needles and all.

FRANKLYN. No, something else has come up –.

HANNAH. Frankie, I don't think this is such a good idea.

FRANKLYN. Honey, we have no choice.

HANNAH. But –.

FRANKLYN. Alison is here.

MARTHA. Oh my God! The college girl you told us about.

FRANKLYN. She just showed up out of the blue an hour ago. And she's willing to sign the contract.

MARTHA. Oh! That's great news! Boy or Girl? Boy or Girl?!

HANNAH. I…I don't know. Forgot to ask.

MARTHA. How could you forget such a thing?

FRANKLYN. But there's a problem. A twist that might stop her from signing.

BEN. Why wouldn't she sign, you're the perfect couple, ask anyone.

FRANKLYN. She doesn't know we're Jewish.

BEN. And you think that might be a deal breaker?

HANNAH. All she knows about Jews is what her father told her.

MARTHA. Which is?

HANNAH. We run Hollywood and killed Jesus.

BEN. Who the hell is her father, Mel Gibson?

FRANKLYN. So were wondering if for the next hour or so, or until she leaves, could you not mention anything Jewish.

BEN. You're kidding.

MARTHA. Is that moral?

FRANKLYN. Well, there are many levels of morality here. And if you are worried about that we could later consult the highest rabbinical authorities on the nuances of our actions but – No! Okay? It's not moral! It's totally immoral!

MARTHA. Hannah, you okay with this?

HANNAH. I don't know. I guess.

FRANKLYN. Martha you gotta help us out. It's nothing complicated, we just can't say or do anything that might lead her to suspect we're Jewish.

MARTHA. Oy!

FRANKLYN. Like that! That's out!

BEN. I won't do it.

FRANKLYN. Ben, you gotta help us. Just until she signs the contract.

BEN. I won't!

HANNAH. Ben, I know this is a little out of the ordinary but we need your help. Please.

BEN. No.

MARTHA. Let me talk to him. Ben, darling, we can do it.

BEN. No.

MARTHA. Sweetheart, when I was a child my father, every Hanukkah would bring us home a dreidel. And he'd spin it. He said that we should realize that where it stops is not a chance thing. Nothing happens by chance. So I'm asking you. Let them find happiness; let's help them take advantage of this. Please.

(**ALISON** *enters with the contract and a pickle.*)

ALISON. Oh, hello.

FRANKLYN. *(overly friendly)* Alison!

HANNAH. *(overly friendly)* Hi!

ALISON. *(a little confused)* Hi.

FRANKLYN. We'd like you to meet two of our best friends.

HANNAH. Yes. This is Ben and Martha.

ALISON. Nice to meet you.

MARTHA. Look at you. How many months along?

ALISON. Seven and a half. You?

MARTHA. Overdue. By any chance, is that a kosher dill –. I mean a pickle?

ALISON. With mustard. Would you like it? I'm sorta full.

MARTHA. I'd love it.

(**ALISON** *hands* **MARTHA** *the pickle.* **MARTHA** *eats. An uncomfortable pause.*)

HANNAH. Well…

FRANKLYN. Yes. Well…

HANNAH. Alison is a freshman at Cal State Northridge. I'm so sorry I forgot your major.

ALISON. Sorta undeclared.

HANNAH. And she's from Iowa.

MARTHA. Iowa? Imagine that.

FRANKLYN. *(desperately trying to make conversation)* Yes… That's the Hawkeye state, isn't it?

ALISON. Yeah. The Hawkeye state.

FRANKLYN. Yeah, she's a Hawkeye all right.

MARTHA. Hawkeye. Imagine that.

(an uncomfortable pause)

MARTHA. We're Lutherans.

ALISON. …Oh.

MARTHA. Yes, we're here to celebrate the eight days of Christmas –

HANNAH. Twelve!

MARTHA. Twelve days. *(mechanical)* As well as the birth of our Lord and savior Jesus Christ.

ALISON. Wow, you celebrate all twelve days?

MARTHA. That's right, Lutherans celebrate all twelve.

ALISON. Really?

MARTHA. Yes, I wish it could be more, but they limit us to twelve.

*(**MARTHA** shoves the picket in her mouth and attempts to genuflect but gets it totally wrong.)*

ALISON. What's that?

MARTHA. It's called a genuflection, dear.

ALISON. Are you sure Lutherans genuflect?

MARTHA. Maybe not in Iowa but it's common here in Van Nuys – am I right? Am I right!

FRANKLYN & HANNAH. Right.

(They attempt to genuflect but also get it all wrong.)

ALISON. You know, The Twelve Days of Christmas is one of my favorite Christmas songs. Once, my high school for its annual Christmas pageant did the whole song with actors. Well, not really actors, just kids from the community. Being Iowa, eight maids a-milking was pretty easy to come by but the ten lords a-leaping sucked. Have you ever seen farm boys leap? Not good.

MARTHA. Our church does a Christmas pageant also. Right before our annual viewing of the *Passion of The Christ.* Isn't that right dear?

BEN. I said I won't do it –.

MARTHA. My husband always plays Scrooge. Say a line from the play for Alison.

*(***BEN*** refuses.)*

MARTHA. Go on. Say a line.

(nothing from **BEN***)*

MARTHA. Say something! Bah. Say, Bah…Bah!

BEN. *(pissed)* Humbug!

ALISON. Wow, that was good. You really embody the character.

MARTHA. That's cause we own a Christmas tree shop.

ALISON. Really?

MARTHA. Yes, a big and tall Christmas tree shop.

ALISON. Wow.

MARTHA. Business is booming.

ALISON. Is that where you get your tree on Christmas Eve?

HANNAH. Sure…Right from Ben's Big and Tall shop.

ALISON. That's way cool.

MARTHA. So, I've heard that you're here to sign a contract.

ALISON. Yes.

MARTHA. I think what you're doing is noble.

ALISON. It isn't easy.

MARTHA. So what happened? Did you pick the perfect couple out of a book at an adoption agency?

ALISON. No, it was a total chance thing.

MARTHA. You don't say.

ALISON. I was just sitting at my aunt's house one night worrying about how I've screwed up my life when the phone rang. I wasn't going to answer it, mostly cause I thought for sure it was my parents. My Dad didn't want me to leave Iowa to go to school. On the spur of the moment I decided I was finally going to tell them the truth. But instead it was Franklyn.

MARTHA. Franklyn? What? Wrong number?

ALISON. No he meant to call. He didn't know who he was calling. He said he was looking for Hannah's hairdresser and then he saw my aunt's name in the phone book –.

BEN. Wait a minute your aunt's name is…?

ALISON. Clara, but she's always been called Happiness.

BEN. Happiness…

ALISON. Hap for short. As a kid she smiled so much her parents nicknamed her Happiness and it kinda stuck. She moved to Northridge thirty years ago to become a holistic doctor – needless to say she's the black sheep of the family. So when I came out here I knew I would be safe. She'd never tell anyone about my…condition.

BEN. *(to FRANKLYN)* …You…called?

FRANKLYN. Yes.

ALISON. And a few moments later I broke down in tears. I don't know why – Just lost it. Crying on the phone to a complete stranger.

FRANKLYN. And before I knew it we had agreed to meet.

HANNAH. Then we had dinner.

ALISON. With chopsticks.

HANNAH. And soon we proposed a solution to all our problems.

MARTHA. Ah. It was one of those completely random coincidences. A strange inexplicable fluke…

ALISON. I guess you could call it that. How did you two meet?

MARTHA. Us? Well, Hannah and I are distant cousins.

FRANKLYN. And Ben and I met in college.

BEN. No, we met before that.

FRANKLYN. We did?

BEN. Yes.

FRANKLYN. No, we were in that history class together.

BEN. No, there was a time before that.

FRANKLYN. There was?

BEN. At the potluck...Remember the potluck?

FRANKLYN. What potluck?

BEN. The potluck...At the Lutheran Church.

FRANKLYN. Oh right, at the Lutheran Church.

(*BEN and* **FRANKLYN** *both genuflect – badly.*)

FRANKLYN. That's right... I forgot.... At Church.

ALISON. I almost feel as if I've known you for my entire life. Sometimes I guess, God answers prayers. By the way, have you thought of a name for her?

HANNAH. (*filled with hope*) Her?

ALISON. Yes, it's a girl. Didn't I tell you that?

HANNAH. ...No.

ALISON. I'm sure you have a wonderful name picked out.

HANNAH. ...Yes. We do...We thought we might name her... Shana Bosha.

ALISON. Shana Bosha – what type of name is that – ?

HANNAH. It's –.

BEN. Swedish!

ALISON. Really?

HANNAH. (*in a Swedish accent*) Ja!

BEN. Yes. Totally Swedish.

BEN/HANNA/MARTHA. (*in a Swedish accent*) Shana Bosha!

ALISON. It's a pretty name. A wonderful name. (*beat*) I'm ready.

FRANKLYN. One contract. And a pen.

(**ALISON** *kneels at the coffee table with the pen and contract.*)

ALISON. Suddenly I feel so calm. I've been debating this for weeks, but now I know in my heart that it's the right thing to do. Here goes.

(*Everyone leans forward in anticipation.* **ALISON** *tries to sign.*)

ALISON. ...Oh dear. Pen's out of ink.

FRANKLYN. I just tested it. Here, Hannah's got one.

ALISON. Thanks.

*(Once again, **ALISON** tries to sign – this pen is also out of ink.)*

ALISON. Nope, no luck.

*(**ALISON** scribbles trying to get it to work.)*

MARTHA. My husband always has a pen. Sweetheart?

*(**MARTHA** grabs a pen from **BEN**'s jacket and hands it to **ALISON**.)*

ALISON. *(reading the side of the pen)* "Ben's Big and Tall – Suits for Less." Suits?

MARTHA. ...That's right. Santa suits.

BEN. Ho ho ho!

ALISON. Oh. Cool. Here goes...

*(**ALISON** leans in to sign.)*

HANNAH. ...Wait!

ALISON. What?

HANNAH. I can't.

FRANKLYN. Hannah...

HANNAH. I can't do it.

ALISON. Something wrong?

HANNAH. Alison, I need to tell you something – Something that might be a deal breaker –

FRANKLYN. What my wife is trying to say is that, we haven't been totally honest.

HANNAH. That's right.

FRANKLYN. The truth is we, on rare occasion, do fight. All couples do. I'm glad I got that off our chest. Shall we?

(The following builds into a fight.)

HANNAH. Frankie –

FRANKLYN. I know sweetheart, everyone says we're the perfect couple.

HANNAH. I want to tell her –

FRANKLYN. I told her. We occasionally fight. *(to* ALISON*)* Are you okay with that? *(to* HANNAH*)* She's okay with that. Let's sign!

HANNAH. Not until – !

FRANKLYN. I told her!

ALISON. Are you two fighting?

FRANKLYN. Oh no, we never fight –

ALISON. But you just said –

HANNAH. I love you Frankie, but shut up....Alison, I hope that we can all be open minded enough to not let this be a problem, but...But...

ALISON. But what?

HANNAH. It's just that... Ben and Martha here are...Jewish.

ALISON. ...Oh.

*(*FRANKLYN *backs away from* BEN *and* MARTHA *in horror.)*

FRANKLYN. Noooooo!

HANNAH. And...Frankie?

FRANKLYN. *(giving up)* ...And so are we.

(beat)

ALISON. ...That would mean that you're not Lutheran.

MARTHA. We're sorta kosher Lutherans –

HANNAH. No. We're not Lutheran at all. Look, Alison, for five years now we've wanted a baby. Five years I've been waiting for that phone to ring and change everything. Sometimes at night I dream that the phone rings and it's Doctor Rosen, or before him Doctor Glenn or before him Doctor Riding, and he tells me that I'm having twins, or triplets. Once it was even septuplets. But then I wake up to reality and the fact that the phone hasn't rung...We've done everything – everything but lie...So if that's a deal breaker, we understand...Well, we don't understand but we won't be upset...Well, we will be upset but we won't say anything...

FRANKLYN. So I guess the question is...Is this a deal breaker?

(**ALISON** *thinks for a moment. She looks at the contract. Pause. She slowly lays the pen down.*

(That little gesture breaks **HANNAH***'s heart.)*

(pause)

ALISON. I guess, I haven't been totally honest with you either. I came to L.A. to get away from my parents. I made a big show about wanting to go to school out here and live with my aunt. But I never started school…Never even applied. I knew I was pregnant. And I knew I had to get as far away from my parents as I could…The baby's father was a nice man. And I want you to know that I was in love with him. At least that night I thought I was…I went to a party in Iowa City that my parents told me not to go to…But then he, the father, left. And I knew he wasn't coming back – He left the country.

FRANKLYN. The country? You told us he went back to the University of Alaska.

ALISON. Um. Yeah.

FRANKLYN. Last time I checked, Alaska is part of the United States.

ALISON. I told you that he went back to U.A. But you interrupted and said University of Alaska before I had a chance to finish. What I meant to say…but you seemed so happy that he was a university boy that I didn't want to bring you down. What I meant to say, before you interrupted, was that he went back to U.A….E.

BEN. …Oh my God.

FRANKLYN. What? University of Alaska at "E". What's a city in Alaska that starts with an "E." Evergreen?

HANNAH. Sweetheart…

FRANKLYN. Help me here.

HANNAH. He didn't go back to Alaska.

FRANKLYN. Where then? *(It hits him)* No…No…

HANNAH. U.A.E.

FRANKLYN. *(dumbfounded)* …United Arab Emirates.

ALISON. He was a transfer student…He went home to U.A.E.

(total silence)

MARTHA. What do you know, another curveball.

*(**ALISON** breaks down in tears.)*

ALISON. …I'm so sorry. I should've told you…My father's right about me. I'm a screw up. All I do is screw things up. I even screwed this up.

MARTHA. No, sweetheart, you're not a screw up. You're just young. *(to **HANNAH**)* Am I right?

HANNAH. Right.

MARTHA. *(to **FRANKLYN**)* Franklyn?

FRANKLYN. Right.

MARTHA. Not a screw up at all. *(to **BEN**)* Am I right?

BEN. No, I think she's pretty much a screw up.

ALISON. So it's a deal breaker?

HANNAH. I…I don't know. Frankie?

FRANKLYN. I don't know…

*(**HANNAH** breaks down in tears.)*

ALISON. I…I think I'll go now…

*(**ALISON** gathers her things and heads for the door.)*

BEN. Wait, it's not the end of the world…Wait maybe it is…

*(Beat. **ALISON** stops at the door.)*

ALISON. I just wanta say that I think you're a really nice couple. And I don't care what religion you are. And I don't want a Mini Cooper convertible…I just want this child to be…to be…loved. Oh!

*(**ALISON** grabs her stomach.)*

ALISON. Oh dear. That's not right.

MARTHA. What is it?

ALISON. Something's happening…Ahhh.

HANNAH. What? What could be happening, you're not due for at least another, what, six weeks!

ALISON. That may be but something's happening.

MARTHA. Does it feel like dull cramps?

ALISON. They're not dull.

MARTHA. In your lower back or pelvis?

ALISON. Both.

MARTHA. Do you have a backache?

ALISON. Since yesterday.

MARTHA. Oh dear, let's get you to the hospital. Ben, you help her! Hannah, help me! Frankie start the car!

(MARTHA throws her keys to FRANKLYN. HANNAH helps MARTHA up. BEN helps ALISON.)

FRANKLYN. *(panicked)* You're kidding. She's, she's, she's –

MARTHA. Start the car!

FRANKLYN. But, but, but –

MARTHA. Start the car!

FRANKLYN. Right, the car!

(FRANKLYN starts for the kitchen/hall.)

MARTHA. We're parked out front!

FRANKLYN. Which way is front?!

HANNAH. That way!

FRANKLYN. Right!

(FRANKLYN runs out.)

MARTHA. Now everyone settle! We're going to be totally calm about this – !

ALISON. Oh dear!

MARTHA. What?

ALISON. I'm wet.

HANNAH. It's okay; the hospital is only a few blocks away.

BEN. Let's go! Move it!

(HANNAH helps ALISON out the door. BEN holds the door for MARTHA.)

MARTHA. Everyone Settle! Just Settle!

(The stage is empty.)

ALISON. *(offstage – overlapping)* Ahhhhhhhhh– !

HANNAH. *(offstage–overlapping)* Deep breaths, deep breaths– !

FRANKLYN. *(offstage – overlapping)* Can't get the door open–

BEN. *(offstage – overlapping)* Use the key– !

FRANKLYN. *(offstage – overlapping)* What key– ?!

HANNAH. *(offstage – overlapping)* The key in your hand– !

FRANKLYN. *(offstage – overlapping)* What hand– ?!

ALISON. *(offstage – overlapping)* Ahhhhhhhh– !

MARTHA. *(offstage – overlapping)* SETTLE– !

ALISON. *(offstage – overlapping)* Ahhhhhhhh– !

BEN. Get in the car! Get in the car– !

MARTHA. *(offstage – overlapping)* EVERYONE SETTLE!

> *(More shouts and panic. We hear the car start up, doors close and it speeds off – horn honking. The lights fade.)*

End of Scene

Scene Two

A Month Later

(The lights rise. The phone rings.)

FRANKLYN. *(offstage)* Coming! It's just Ben and Martha calling to tell us they're going to be late. I got it.

(FRANKLYN runs in and answers the phone.)

FRANKLYN. *(on the phone)* Hey there. Stuck in traffic? … Oh, hello…I didn't expect you to call, Rabbi Marks… It's not Purim…Really, you don't say. When did this occur?…That's great news. I'm thrilled that you can walk again…Yes…I'm glad that it allowed you to slow down and see life with new eyes, but Rabbi Marks, I'm not sure that me running you down in a crosswalk would qualify as part of God's plan.

(doorbell)

FRANKLYN. *(on the phone)* …Sure I guess I see your point… Could I call you back? …Friends are coming over… Really? You're off to Hawaii.

(two doorbells)

FRANKLYN. Well, thank you for calling…What?…Yes, I guess that now that you're better we could come back to temple…I'll talk to you soon…Yes…Aloha.

(FRANKLYN hangs up and answers the door. BEN enters.)

FRANKLYN. Ben!

BEN. Franklyn.

(They hug.)

BEN. Are you ready? I present to you the next Big and Tall King of L.A.!

(MARTHA enters pushing a baby carriage. MARTHA and BEN hug, they coo over the baby.)

FRANKLYN. He looks just like you.

BEN. Yes, he does have my charm. *(to the baby)* Max, can you say hello to Uncle Frankie?

FRANKLYN. Hello Max.

MARTHA. "Hello" may be a few months off.

BEN. Don't be so sure, he has my mouth, he could start talking any day now.

(HANNAH enters with a plate of snacks and places it on the table.)

HANNAH. Hellooooo! *(seeing the baby)* There's my little man. What a perfect boy. And so big. Goochie Goo.

(They all coo over the baby.)

FRANKLYN. And *we* got something to show you.

MARTHA. I'm sure you do.

FRANKLYN. Right back.

(FRANKLYN runs into the kitchen/hall. BEN, MARTHA and HANNAH continue to coo over the baby.)

MARTHA. Have you heard from Alison?

HANNAH. Yes – Goochie Goo – she went back to Iowa. She calls once a month to say hello. Matter of fact she should be calling any minute.

(FRANKLYN pokes just his head in. We can see that he has something in his arms.)

FRANKLYN. Are you ready!

BEN & MARTHA. We're ready!

FRANKLYN. Here goes!

(FRANKLYN enters with his manuscript.)

FRANKLYN. Finished it. Two hundred and fifty two pages. Not a soul is interested in publishing it but I don't care. I just had to prove that I could do it.

(an offstage bing)

HANNAH. Oh, that's the oven.

(HANNAH exits.)

BEN. No publisher?

FRANKLYN. Nothing but rejections.

BEN. If you're interested, I know this head doctor who specializes in unpublished authors.

FRANKLYN. No. I've sorta given up on that. It's, if I may be totally honest, pretty bad.

MARTHA. If you think that then why did you write it?

FRANKLYN. To prove to myself that I wasn't a writer. I got my old job back.

MARTHA. With Hannah's father?

FRANKLYN. It's not that bad. And I do have a lot of job security. And free legal advice anytime I need it. And it makes Hannah happy.

BEN. You're the perfect couple, did you know that? Martha and I are always saying, you're macaroni and cheese, do we not say that all the time?

MARTHA. All the time.

FRANKLYN. Perhaps we are.

MARTHA. And you have so much to be thankful for, in spite of everything.

FRANKLYN. Yes. In spite of everything.

(*HANNAH enters holding a baby.*)

MARTHA. Ahhhhhh! There she is!

(*They gather around the babies. Everyone cooing and making faces.*)

MARTHA. She's perfect, is she not perfect?

BEN. Perfect. But so small.

HANNAH. Doctor says she's doing well. Gaining weight.

MARTHA. So tell me. With all the problems what have you decided?

HANNAH. Decided?

MARTHA. What're you going to raise her? I mean, you know, the whole thing with the mother…and the father.

HANNAH. Oh…That's easy. We've decided that we're going to raise her to be honest, to study a lot and not to be hateful – to herself or to others. And above all – to be ready for a few curveballs.

BEN. That's the whole shebang isn't it – the rest is just commentary.

MARTHA. Shabat Shalom.

BEN & HANNAH & FRANKLYN. Shabat Shalom.

(The phone rings.)

HANNAH. That's Alison.

(HANNAH answers.)

HANNAH. Hello – How are things in Iowa –. Oh, Dr. Rosen. ...No. You're not bothering us. We're having a lovely evening, just family, friends and good conversation... What? ...If it's okay, I'd rather take the news standing up. *(beat)* ...Well, that's certainly unexpected...Thank you.

(Stunned, she slowly hangs up.)

FRANKLYN. Sweetheart what is it?

MARTHA. What? Tell us.

HANNAH. How's this for a curveball –.

(But before she can tell them...)

(blackout)

The End

PROPS LIST

GENERAL

Dinner setting
Wine glasses
Wine opener
Business cards
Several pens
A novel manuscript
A Jewish Purim Gragger (Noisemaker)
A legal looking contract
A page from the white pages of a telephone book
A long measuring tape
A menorah
A college student's backpack
A small stuffed Santa Claus
A baby in a blanket
A baby in a baby carriage
Car keys
A Mezuzah

FOOD

Large Pickles
Whipped Cream
Mustard
Nuts
Several bottles of white wine
Haman's Pockets, chips, dip, popcorn and other before dinner snacks.

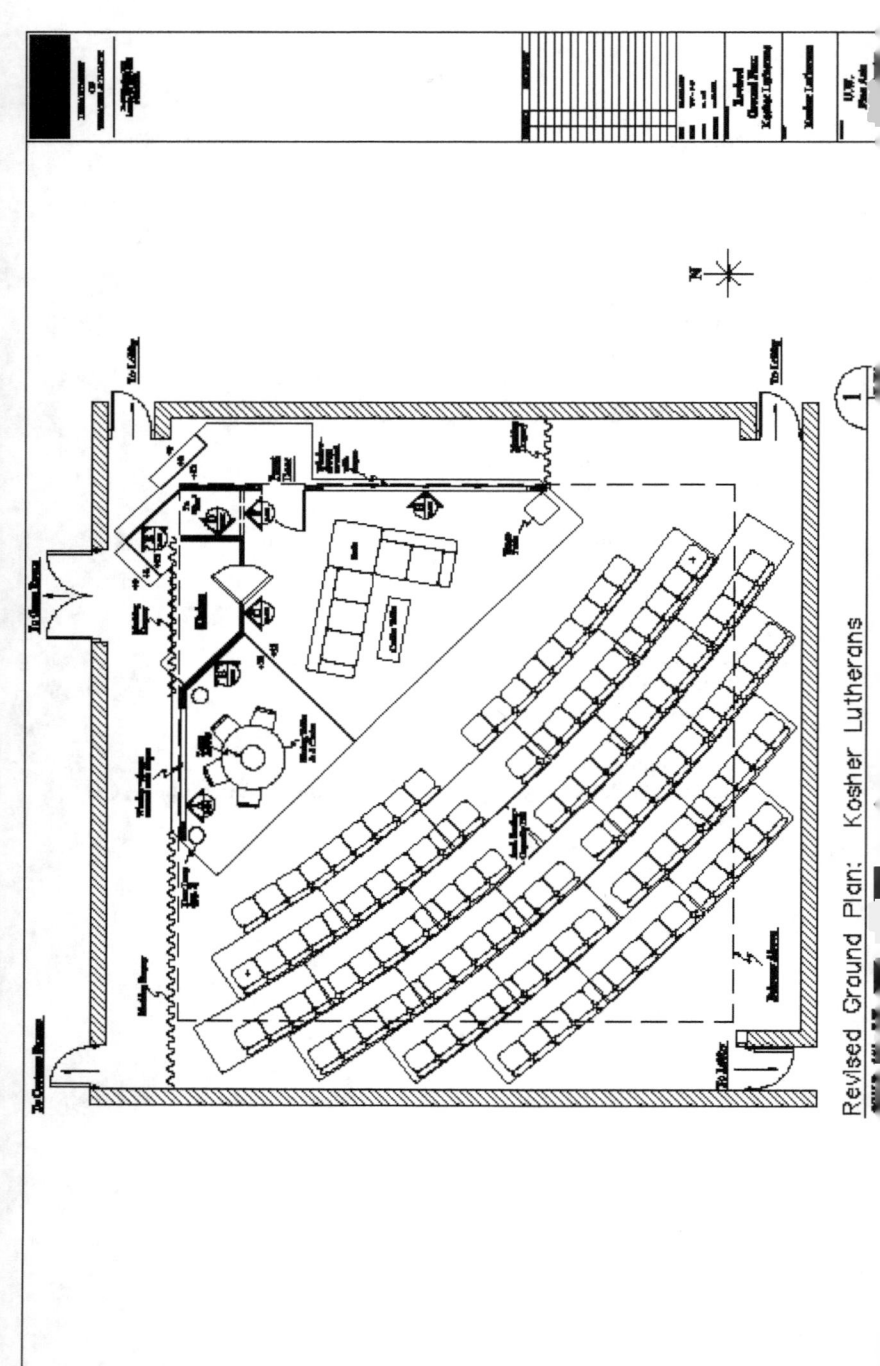

Revised Ground Plan: Kosher Lutherans

Perspective Sketch: *Kosher Lutherans*

Not to Scale

Designed by Mike Earl

OTHER TITLES AVAILABLE FROM SAMUEL FRENCH

COCKEYED
William Missouri Downs

Comedy

3m, 1w

Unit Set

Winner of the HotCity Theatre GreenHouse New Play Festival

Phil, an average nice guy, is madly in love with the beautiful Sophia. The only problem is that she's unaware of his existence. He tries to introduce himself but she looks right through him. When Phil discovers Sophia has a glass eye, he thinks that might be the problem, but soon realizes that she really can't see him. Perhaps he is caught in a philosophical hyperspace or dualistic reality or perhaps beautiful women are just unaware of nice guys. Armed only with a B.A. in philosophy, Phil sets out to prove his existence and win Sophia's heart. This fast moving farce is the winner of the HotCity Theatre's GreenHouse New Play Festival. *The St. Louis Post-Dispatch* called *Cockeyed* a clever romantic comedy, *Talkin' Broadway* called it "hilarious," while *Playback Magazine* said that it was "fresh and invigorating."

"Rocking with laughter...hilarious...polished and engaging work draws heavily on the age-old conventions of farce: improbable situations, exaggerated characters, amazing coincidences, absurd misunderstandings, people hiding in closets and barely missing each other as they run in and out of doors...full of comic momentum as *Cockeyed* hurtles toward its conclusion."
- *Talkin' Broadway*

OTHER TITLES AVAILABLE FROM SAMUEL FRENCH

SECRETS OF A SOCCER MOM
Kathleen Clark

Full Length, Comedy / 3 f / Exterior

Three engaging women reluctantly take the field in a mothers vs. sons soccer game. They intend to let the children win, but as the game unfolds they become intent on scoring. The competition ignites a fierce desire to recapture their youthful good-humor, independence and sexiness, paving the way toward a better understanding of themselves, their families and changes they need to make in their lives.

"Let's hear it for *Soccer Moms,* a diverting comedy with a slick style and attention, holding crisp dialogue."
-The New York Times

"A sympathetic and compelling comedy with constant laughs."
- Variety

"Soccer moms of the world, unite and jog over to enjoy Kathleen Clark's new comedy."
- Associated Press

"*Secrets of A Soccer Mom* puts the heart and 'sole' into comedy."
- New York Daily News